Alfred A . Knopf 🐎 **New York**

BUNNY

JENNIFER GRAY OLSON

Rule 1: A super awesome ninja must always work

alone.

...especially in the most dangerous of situations.

A super awesome ninja must:

Rule 3: possess incredible strength.

Rule 4: achieve invisibility.

Rule 5: create ninja weapons.

Rule 6: know how to escape!

Rule 7:
become
skilled
at climbing.

Rule 8:
maintain
perfect
balance.

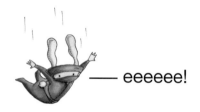— eeeeee!

Rule 9:
master
the ability
to fly.

Rule 10: A super awesome ninja must battle anyone anywhere anytime

alone.

— uh-oh.

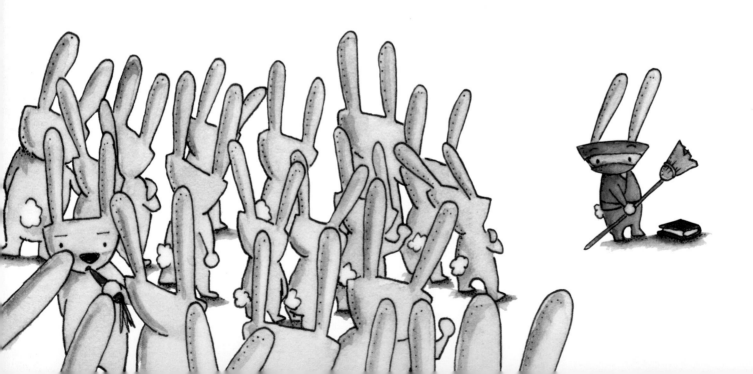

uh-oh. ——

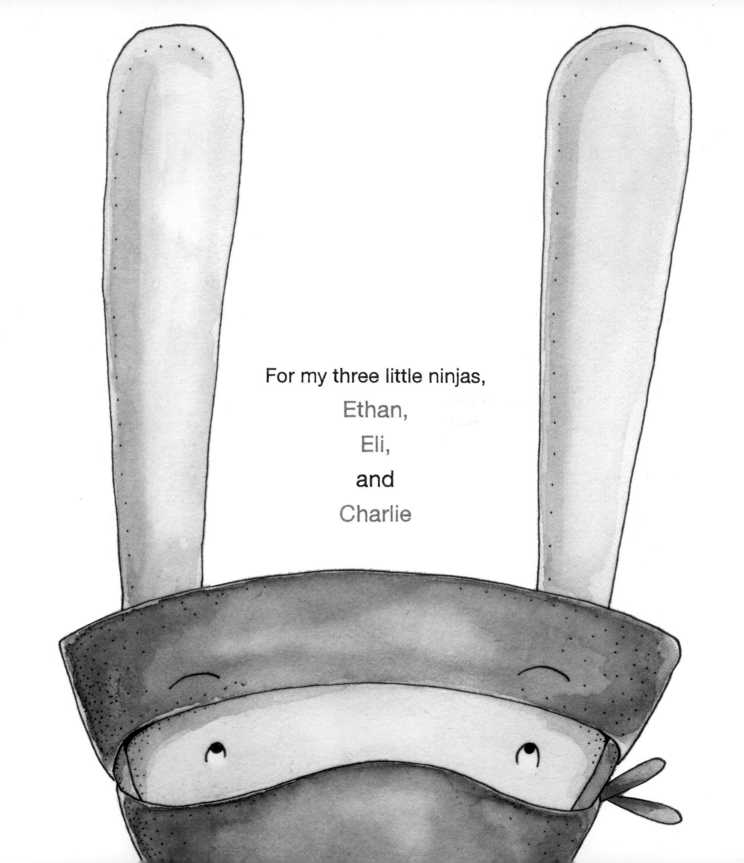

For my three little ninjas,

Ethan,

Eli,

and

Charlie

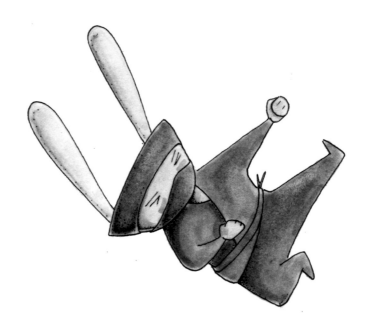

THIS IS A BORZOI BOOK PUBLISHED BY ALFRED A. KNOPF

Copyright © 2015 by Jennifer Gray Olson

All rights reserved. Published in the United States by Alfred A. Knopf, an imprint of Random House Children's Books,

a division of Random House LLC, a Penguin Random House Company, New York.

Knopf, Borzoi Books, and the colophon are registered trademarks of Random House LLC.

Visit us on the Web! randomhouse.com/kids

Educators and librarians, for a variety of teaching tools, visit us at RHTeachersLibrarians.com

Library of Congress Cataloging-in-Publication Data

Olson, Jennifer Gray.

Ninja bunny / by Jennifer Gray Olson, author, illustrator — 1st ed.

p.   cm.

Summary: A little rabbit tries to follow the rules in order to become a "super awesome ninja,"

but discovers that his book is wrong about one very important thing.

ISBN 978-0-385-75493-4 (trade) — ISBN 978-0-385-75494-1 (lib. bdg.) — ISBN 978-0-385-75495-8 (ebook)

[1. Ninjas—Fiction. 2. Rabbits—Fiction. 3. Friendship—Fiction.] I. Title.

PZ7.O5196 Nin 2015 [E]—dc23 2014004220

The illustrations in this book were created using ink and watercolor.

MANUFACTURED IN CHINA

June 2015   10 9 8 7 6 5 4 3 2   First Edition

Random House Children's Books supports the First Amendment and celebrates the right to read.